PUNCTUATION
Takes a Vacation

by
ROBIN PULVER

Illustrated by
LYNN ROWE REED

Holiday House / New York

Library of Congress Cataloging-in-Publication Data

Pulver, Robin.
Punctuation takes a vacation/by Robin Pulver;
illustrated by Lynn Rowe Reed.—1st ed.
p. cm.
Summary: When all the punctuation marks in
Mr. Wright's class decide to take a vacation, the students
discover just how difficult life can be without them.

ISBN 0–8234–1687–9 (hardcover)

ISBN 0–8234–1820–0 (paperback)

[1. Punctuation—Fiction. 2. Schools—Fiction.]
I. Reed, Lynn Rowe, ill. II. Title.

PZ7.P97325 Pu 2003
[Fic]—dc21   2002068915

ISBN-13: 978-0-8234-1687-5 (hardcover)   ISBN-10: 0-8234-1687-9 (hardcover)
ISBN-13: 978-0-8234-1820-6 (paperback)   ISBN-10: 0-8234-1820-0 (paperback)

For Seth:
You popped the question?
Hooray!
Wishing you and Nina
a meaningful, joyful life together,
punctuated with perfect vacations.
Don't forget to send postcards!

Special thanks to Cindy Kane

R. P.

To Lael and Dan

L. R. R.

Day after day, the punctuation marks showed up in Mr. Wright's classroom.
Day after day, they did their jobs.

They put up with
being erased
and replaced
and corrected
and ignored
and moved around.

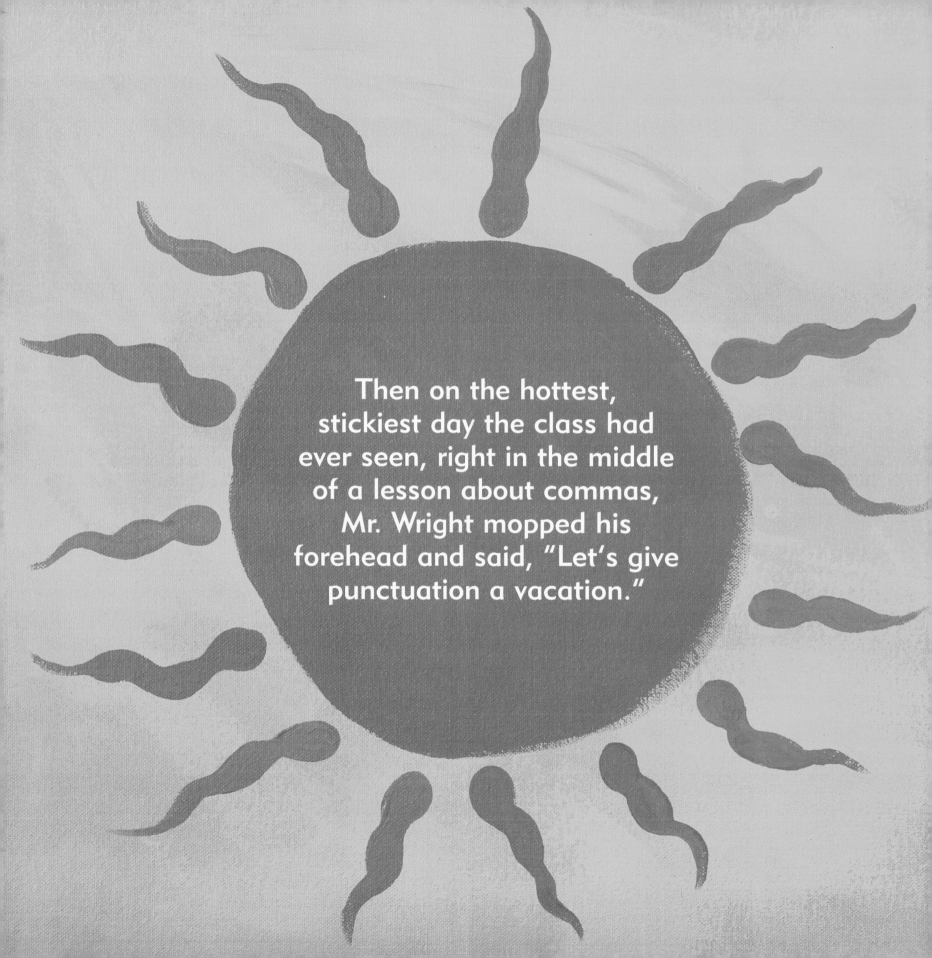

Then on the hottest, stickiest day the class had ever seen, right in the middle of a lesson about commas, Mr. Wright mopped his forehead and said, "Let's give punctuation a vacation."

As the kids
cheered and
headed for
the playground
to cool off,

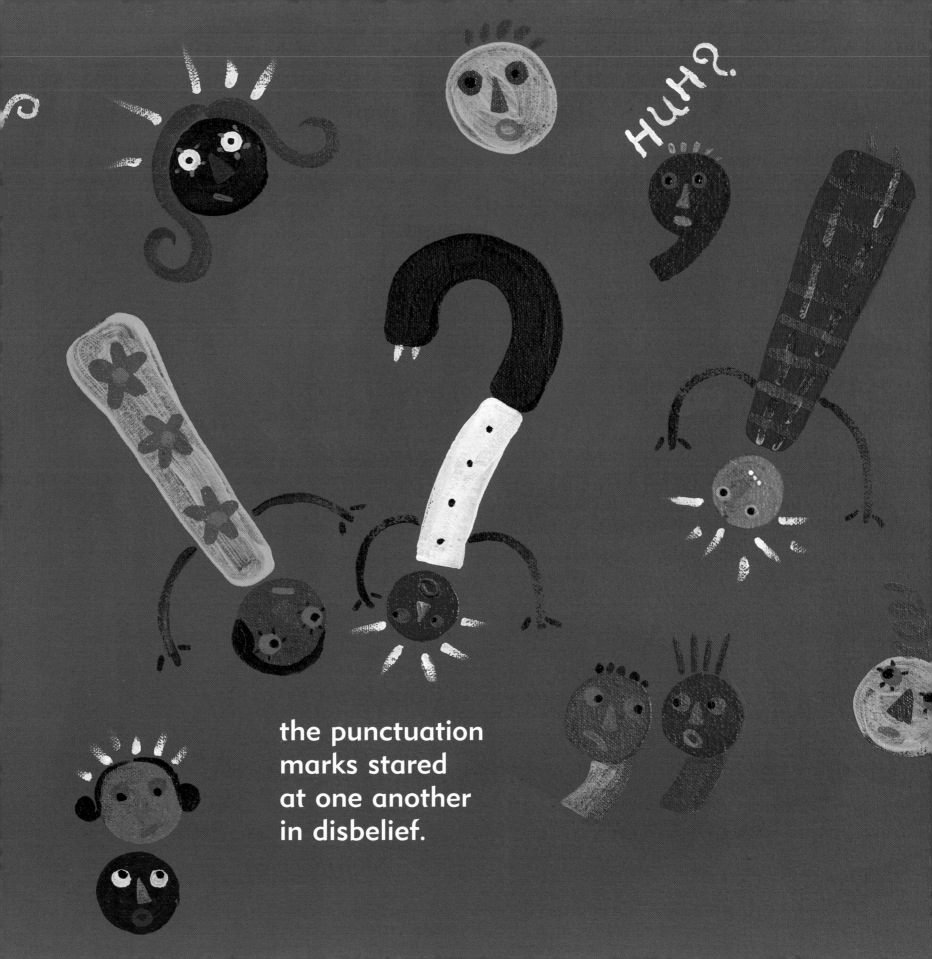

the punctuation marks stared at one another in disbelief.

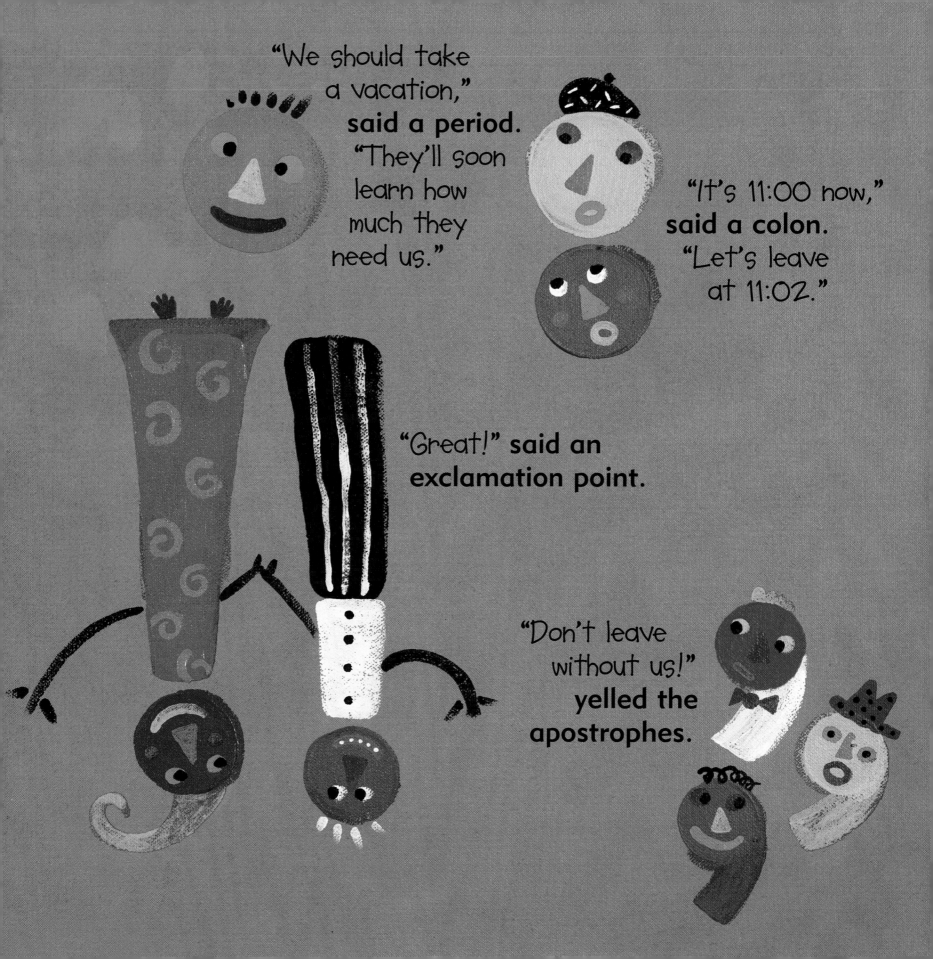

out the door.

Whoosh!
They rushed back in to
grab the quotation marks,
who were too busy talking
to pay attention.

When Mr. Wright's class returned from the playground, they couldn't wait to find out what happened in Chapter 4 of their book, *Ace Scooper, Dog Detective*.

Mr. Wright opened his mouth to read aloud, but then he stopped and stared.

Mr. Wright was right. Nothing made sense without punctuation.

Do you miss us?
How much?
Why couldn't we take a vacation sooner?
Guess who?

Mr. Wright's class
Hometown
USA 46738

A couple days later, the school secretary delivered a small bundle of postcards to Mr. Wright's class. They were postmarked "Take-a-Break Lake."

We flop. We plop. We stop. We stay put in our lounge chairs. We are happy thinking our complete thoughts.
Thoughtfully yours,
Sentence Stoppers

Mr. Wright's class
Hometown
USA 46738

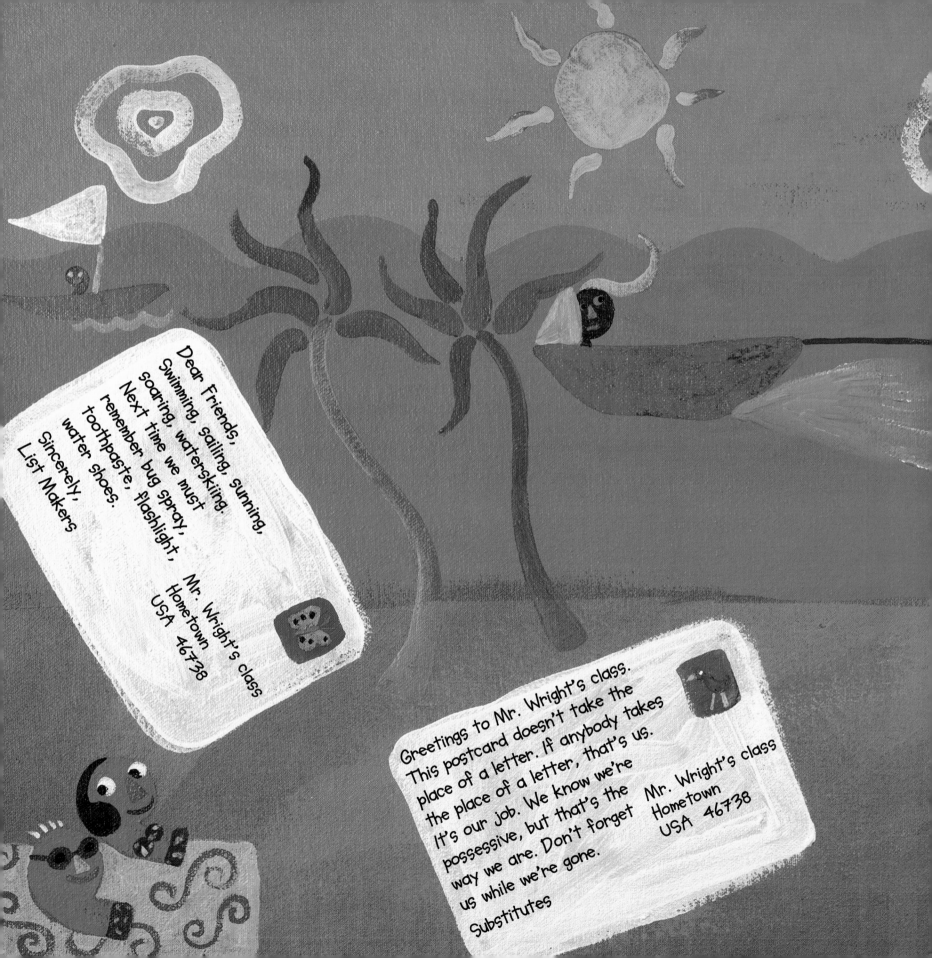

The kids guessed
who wrote the postcards,
and they wanted to write back.
But they couldn't write
without punctuation.

The best they could do
was borrow some from
Mr. Rongo's class next door,
where punctuation seemed
to be running wild.

Dear, Punctuation

Please come! back We need you?
We, miss, you, too. Life at? school
is! "difficult" without, you?

We can?t do reading writing or
riddles? without punctuation
Chapter 4 of our book *Ace, Scooper,*
does,nt make sense We, will, never?
take punctuation for! granted
again. Wont you please come back
before 10 00 on Friday:

Mr Wright says. Punctuation,
please come home

Sincerely

Mr' Wright.s Class

Mr' Wright.s Class

Punctuation
Take-a-Break Lake

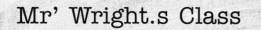

URGENT!

HURRY!

NO.2 PENCIL

So the punctuation marks returned to Mr. Wright's classroom to do the jobs only they could do.

Mr. Rongo's unruly punctuation scrambled back to their own classroom.

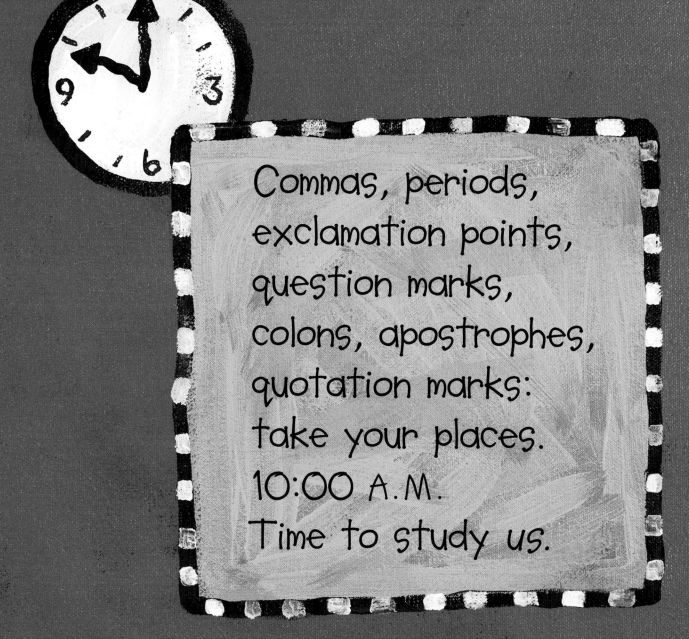

Commas, periods,
exclamation points,
question marks,
colons, apostrophes,
quotation marks:
take your places.
10:00 A.M.
Time to study us.

HOORAY FOR PUNCTUATION!

the end.

PUNCTUATION RULES!

Quotation marks belong at the beginning and end of words a person speaks.

The **question mark** comes at the end of a question.

Use a **comma** to separate each item in a series or list. A comma also separates two complete thoughts in a sentence.

Use an **exclamation point** after a word or sentence that expresses strong feelings.

An **apostrophe** takes the place of a letter and changes two words into one word. An apostrophe is used with the letter *s* to show ownership or possession.

The **colon** lets you know what time it is. It separates the big guys (hours) from the little guys (minutes).

The **period** is the stop sign at the end of a sentence or complete thought. It is also used in abbreviations.

Punctuation marks work together to make reading and writing flow smoothly.

Mr. Wright said, "Thank you very much!" when we gave him a T-shirt from Take-a-Break Lake.

Did anybody find my missing flip-flop? Where, oh, where could it be?

That's Question Mark's flip-flop? I didn't know. It's in my suitcase.

I collected shells, stones, blisters, pinecones, feathers, and bug bites. It was fun, but I am SO tired.

Hey! Look! Great photos of us at Take-a-Break Lake!

Gosh, it's 2:15. Time to return the library book I took on vacation.

This photo is of me. I stopped two sentences from crashing into each other at the corner of Bay St. and Lake Ave.